With special thanks to the
SpongeBob SquarePants writers

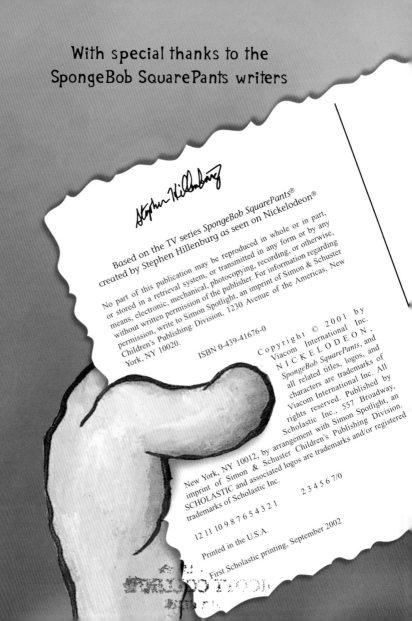

Based on the TV series *SpongeBob SquarePants*®
created by Stephen Hillenburg as seen on Nickelodeon®

No part of this publication may be reproduced in whole or in part,
or stored in a retrieval system, or transmitted in any form or by any
means, electronic, mechanical, photocopying, recording, or otherwise,
without written permission of the publisher. For information regarding
permission, write to Simon Spotlight, an imprint of Simon & Schuster
Children's Publishing Division, 1230 Avenue of the Americas, New
York, NY 10020.

ISBN 0-439-41676-0

Copyright © 2001 by
Viacom International Inc.
NICKELODEON,
SpongeBob SquarePants, and
all related titles, logos, and
characters are trademarks of
Viacom International Inc. All
rights reserved. Published by
Scholastic Inc., 557 Broadway,
New York, NY 10012, by arrangement with Simon Spotlight, an
imprint of Simon & Schuster Children's Publishing Division.
SCHOLASTIC and associated logos are trademarks and/or registered
trademarks of Scholastic Inc.

12 11 10 9 8 7 6 5 4 3 2 1   2 3 4 5 6 7/0

Printed in the U.S.A.

First Scholastic printing, September 2002

Greetings From Bikini Bottom

SCHOLASTIC INC.

New York   Toronto   London   Auckland   Sydney
Mexico City   New Delhi   Hong Kong   Buenos Aires

Diane M. Halle Library
ENDICOTT COLLEGE
Beverly, MA 01915

Bikini Bottom,

where some of the

finest specimens of

underwater life

can be found . . .

Good Morning, Bikini Bottom!

Ah! What a bee-yoo-tiful day!

We're gonna make this your . . . *best day ever!*

Bubble Blowing Is Serious Business in Bikini Bottom

1 First we go like this . . .
   spin around!

2 Double-take three
   times . . . one, two,
   and three, then . . .

3 Pelvic thrust—
   Whoo-oooo-whoo!

4 Stomp on your right
   Foot. Don't Forget it!

5 Now it's time to bring it around town. Go ahead, BRING IT AROUND TOWN!

6 Then you do this, then this, then this, and this and that and thisandthatandthisandthatandthisandthat!

Go, SpongeBob!
Go, SpongeBob!
Go, self!

PATRiCK and SPONGEBOB

Man Sponge and Boy Patrick!
To the invisible boatmobile!

SPONGEBOB: WAiT! I don't have a license.
PATRiCK: Well, this is an invisible boat . . . so you need an invisible license!
SPONGEBOB: You're the best sidekick ever.

SQUIDWARD TENTACLES

Oh, my aching tentacles!

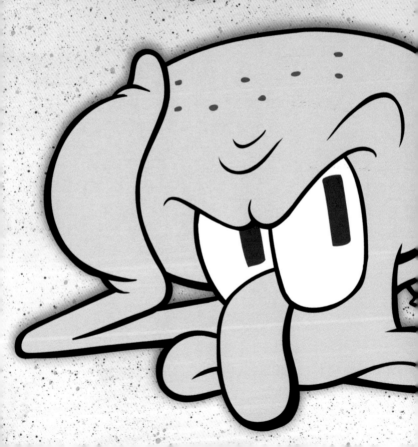

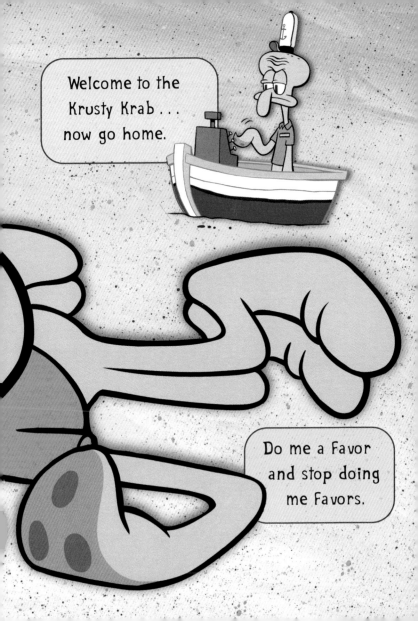

GARY

Meow.

Meow?

MEOW!

SANDY CHEEKS

SANDY: I like you, SpongeBob. We could be tighter than bark on a tree.
SPONGEBOB: I like you, too, Sandy. Say, what's that thing on your head?

MR. KRABS

Do you smell it? I smell the smelly smell of something that smells smelly.

Ahh, it warms my wallet to see my employees coming in early.

Attention! All Krusty Krab employees— attention! Get the anchors out of your pants and report to my office! That will be all.

Who stole the Krabby Patty?

Clues:
1. Has a tough time picking out glasses
2. Is in the restaurant business
3. Is a college graduate
4. Evil

*The Krabby Patty formula is the sole property of the Krusty Krab and is only to be discussed in part or in whole with its creator, Mr. Krabs. Duplication of this formula is punishable by law. Restrictions apply, results may vary.

Wherever there is a secret recipe, there is someone who wants to steal it. . . .

Answer: Plankton

PLANKTON

It's becoming increasingly obvious. I can deny it no longer... I am small.

Oh, Bikini Bottom, we pledge our hearts to you. As faithful, as deep, as true, as blue, oh, Bikini Bottom, we love you!

Run along now, you don't belong down here with us bottom feeders!

ENDICOTT COLLEGE

Juv
Fic
Spo

Diane M. Halle Library
ENDICOTT COLLEGE
Beverly, MA 01915